America's Leaders

THE
Secretary of
DEFENSE

by Scott Ingram

BLACKBIRCH PRESS

San Diego • Detroit • New York • San Francisco • Cleveland • New Haven, Conn. • Waterville, Maine • London • Munich

© 2002 by Blackbirch Press™. Blackbirch Press™ is an imprint of The Gale Group, Inc., a division of Thomson Learning, Inc.

Blackbirch Press™ and Thomson Learning™ are trademarks used herein under license.

For more information, contact
The Gale Group, Inc.
27500 Drake Rd.
Farmington Hills, MI 48331-3535
Or you can visit our Internet site at http://www.gale.com

ALL RIGHTS RESERVED
No part of this work covered by the copyright hereon may be reproduced or used in any form or by any means—graphic, electronic, or mechanical, including photocopying, recording, taping, Web distribution or information storage retrieval systems—without the written permission of the publisher.

Every effort has been made to trace the owners of copyrighted material.

Photo credits: cover background, back cover, pages 3, 4, 6, 8, 10, 12, 14, 15, 20, 22, 26, 28, 30-31, 32 © Creatas; Marshall cover inset and McNamara cover inset, pages 7, 8, 9, 11, 17, 19, 21, 22, 23, 24, 25, 28, 29 © CORBIS; pages 5, 6, 12, 14, 15, 16, 20, 27, 29 © Department of Defense; page 18 © Library of Congress

LIBRARY OF CONGRESS CATALOGING-IN-PUBLICATION DATA

Ingram, Scott.
  The Secretary of Defense / by W. Scott Ingram.
    p. cm. — (America's leaders series)
  Summary: Takes a thorough look at the Secretary of Defense of the United States, including the history of the office, how the work relates to that of other government offices, and how Secretaries have handled crises.
  ISBN 1-56711-666-3 (hardback)
  1. United States. Dept. of Defense. Office of the Secretary of Defense—Juvenile literature. [1. United States. Dept. of Defense. Office of the Secretary of Defense.] I. Title. II. Series.
    UA23.6 .I53 2003
    355.6'0973—dc21   2002003525

Printed in United States
10 9 8 7 6 5 4 3 2 1

Table of Contents

The Nation's Chief Military Adviser 4

The Secretary's Responsibilities 8

Who Works with the Secretary? 12

Where Does the Secretary Work? 14

Requirements for Secretary .18

Steps to Approval 20

Doing the Job 21

A Time of Crisis 22

A Secretary's Day 26

Fascinating Facts 28

Glossary 30

For More Information 31

Index 32

The Nation's Chief Military Adviser

More than 200 years ago, a group of men wrote a document, the U.S. Constitution, which established the American government. The authors of the Constitution divided the government into 3 separate branches, the legislative branch, the judicial branch, and the executive branch. Under the Constitution, the leader of the executive branch was the president.

Ever since the first president, George Washington, took office, presidents have had people to advise them. In 1789, the U.S. Congress voted to establish departments in the executive branch to assist the president. These were the departments of state, treasury, and war. The leader of each department was called a secretary, and together the secretaries formed a group of advisers known as the president's cabinet.

The Constitution also gave the president the title of commander in chief of the U.S. armed forces. For more than 150 years, the nation's armed forces were made up of the army and the navy. The secretary of war was

Secretary of Defense Donald Rumsfeld (right) holds a press conference with General Richard B. Meyers at his side.

in charge of the nation's army, and the secretary of the navy—a position established in 1798—was in charge of the navy. Both were cabinet members.

The president is the commander in chief of the U.S. armed forces. The secretary of defense is his chief military adviser.

In 1947, a new branch of the armed forces, the United States Air Force, was created by Congress. Instead of creating a separate cabinet position, U.S. lawmakers established the department of defense

USA Fact
In 2002, the annual salary of the secretary of defense was $161,200.

as part of the executive branch and put all 3 services under a secretary of defense. In 1949, the position of secretary of defense became a cabinet position. The

secretary of defense is now the chief adviser to the president on military and defense issues.

In 1947, Congress also created a special section of the executive branch called the National Security Council (NSC). The secretary of defense is a member of the NSC, which advises the president on national security and foreign policy matters. The other members of the council, in addition to the president and secretary of defense, are the vice president, the secretary of state, the secretary of the treasury, and the national security adviser.

President Ronald Reagan meets with Secretary of Defense Caspar Weinberger (third from left) and other members of his National Security Council.

The Secretary's Responsibilities

The Department of Defense was established to "provide the military forces needed to deter [prevent] war and to protect the security of our country." The department includes all the branches of the armed services. It also includes 15 defense agencies. Defense agencies handle

Weapons, such as guided missiles, are developed and purchased by the Defense Department.

Secretary of Defense Donald Rumsfeld speaks to members of the armed forces about matters of national defense.

responsibilities such as weapons research and development. They also handle supply purchases, finances, and military life issues. The secretary of defense is the leader of the department and its agencies.

The Defense Department has more than 1.5 million men and women on active duty in the armed forces as well as 1.2 million reserves and more than 650,000 civilian employees—a total of more than 3 million people. The secretary of defense is the leader of the men and women who defend the United States.

Each year, the Defense Department submits a budget to the president as part of the budget for the entire government. Almost half of the money in the defense budget is used to pay members of the military and defense employees. A large percentage is used to keep jets, missiles, ships, and ground vehicles ready for service. Part of the budget is set aside to buy or develop new weapons. The secretary of defense prepares the department's budget and presents it to the president.

As a cabinet member, the secretary advises the president on defense issues. These issues may include items in the budget, development of new weapons systems, the use of American forces in foreign countries, and matters of national security.

USA Fact

The 4 armed services are the air force, army, navy, and marines. The marines are part of the Naval Service. A fifth armed service, the Coast Guard, operates under command of the Transportation Department during peacetime but under navy control during wartime.

Part of the defense budget is used to keep fighter jets ready for service.

In budget matters, the secretary of defense is also responsible to the legislative branch of the government. The U.S. Congress—both the Senate and the House of Representatives—must review and approve all programs of the Defense Department. The secretary appears before both the House and Senate Armed Services Committees to discuss defense issues and expenses.

Who Works with the Secretary?

Just as the president needs advisers to help run the executive branch, the secretary needs advisers in the Defense Department. Some advisers work in the office of the secretary of defense. They include the deputy secretary of defense, whose job is similar to that of the vice president. The deputy secretary stands in for the secretary whenever it is necessary and has all of the same powers. Reporting to the secretary and deputy secretary are heads of individual agencies known by titles such as assistant secretary and undersecretary. These men and women handle defense issues such as housing, finances, legal matters, weapons development, purchases, missile defense, and other military matters.

The Joint Chiefs of Staff are the top-ranking officers in the armed forces.

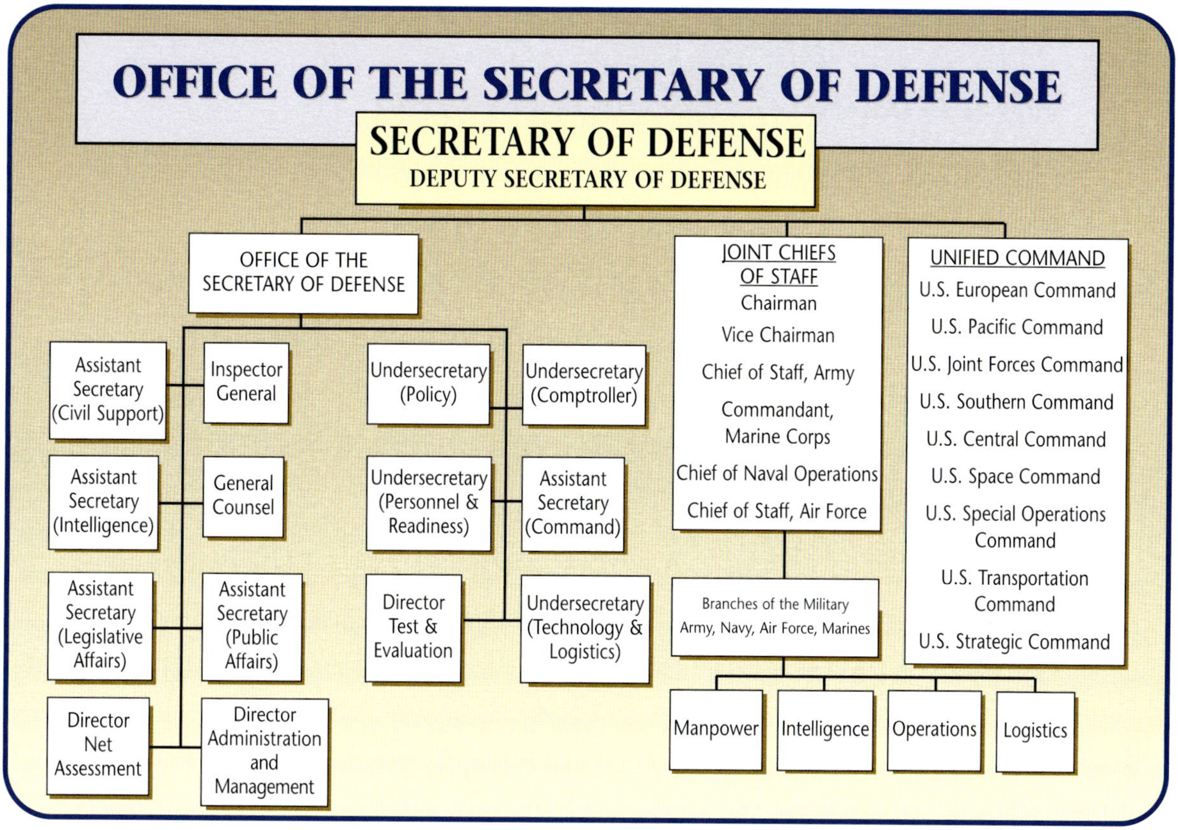

OFFICE OF THE SECRETARY OF DEFENSE

SECRETARY OF DEFENSE
DEPUTY SECRETARY OF DEFENSE

OFFICE OF THE SECRETARY OF DEFENSE
- Assistant Secretary (Civil Support)
- Assistant Secretary (Intelligence)
- Assistant Secretary (Legislative Affairs)
- Director Net Assessment
- Inspector General
- General Counsel
- Assistant Secretary (Public Affairs)
- Director Administration and Management
- Undersecretary (Policy)
- Undersecretary (Personnel & Readiness)
- Director Test & Evaluation
- Undersecretary (Comptroller)
- Assistant Secretary (Command)
- Undersecretary (Technology & Logistics)

JOINT CHIEFS OF STAFF
- Chairman
- Vice Chairman
- Chief of Staff, Army
- Commandant, Marine Corps
- Chief of Naval Operations
- Chief of Staff, Air Force

Branches of the Military
Army, Navy, Air Force, Marines
- Manpower
- Intelligence
- Operations
- Logistics

UNIFIED COMMAND
- U.S. European Command
- U.S. Pacific Command
- U.S. Joint Forces Command
- U.S. Southern Command
- U.S. Central Command
- U.S. Space Command
- U.S. Special Operations Command
- U.S. Transportation Command
- U.S. Strategic Command

The Defense Department is the largest department in the executive branch.

The secretary also has assistance from the armed services in operating the department. The main group reporting to the secretary is known as the Joint Chiefs of Staff. The 6 members of the joint chiefs are the top-ranking officers from the 4 armed services.

Reporting to the joint chiefs and the secretary of defense are the top-ranking military officers of the Unified Commands. Those officers are in charge of all military operations within certain geographic areas such as Europe, the Pacific, or regions within the United States. There is no set number of members for the Unified Commands.

Where Does the Secretary Work?

The office of the secretary of defense is in the Pentagon, a 5-sided office building in Arlington, Virginia. The Pentagon is among the largest office buildings in the world. It has 3 times more floor space than the Empire State Building in New York City. The entire Capitol building could fit into any of the 5 sections of the Pentagon.

In addition to the secretary, more than 23,000 other civilians and military staff work at the Pentagon. These people make over 200,000 phone calls every day, using more than 100,000 miles of telephone line in the building. One amazing fact about the Pentagon is that it has 17.5 miles of hallways, yet, because of its shape, it never takes more than 7 minutes to walk between any 2 points.

The president sometimes meets the secretary and other national security advisers at the Pentagon.

14

The Pentagon is located across the Potomac River from Washington, D.C.

USA Fact

Construction of the Pentagon began on September 11, 1941. Exactly 60 years later, on September 11, 2001, terrorists flew a hijacked passenger jet into the Pentagon, killing 198 people and destroying a section of the building. Defense secretary Donald Rumsfeld was in his office at the time of the attack. Unharmed, he helped to rescue people trapped at the crash area.

President George W. Bush and Secretary of Defense Donald Rumsfeld view the Pentagon after the terrorist attack.

The White House and Capitol

As a member of the cabinet, the secretary of defense meets often with the president. The secretary may meet in the president's main working area, the Oval Office. During cabinet meetings, the secretary meets with other members and the president in the cabinet meeting room, a few steps from the Oval Office.

The secretary of defense often appears at the U.S. Capitol before congressional committees.

The secretary often travels abroad to meet defense ministers from other countries.

Secretary of Defense Richard Cheney shakes hands with a Saudi Arabian military officer in Kuwait during Operation Desert Storm in 1991.

Outside of Washington

It is not unusual for the secretary to travel to military bases in or out of the United States. A secretary may also meet with defense ministers of other countries to discuss military operations or agreements.

Requirements for Secretary

In 1947, the U.S. Congress passed the National Security Act, which created the Department of Defense under the supervision of the secretary of defense. Government leaders felt that it was important to place a civilian in control of the nation's military so that all services were treated equally in budget and other matters. The National Security Act forbids a commissioned military officer who has been on active duty within the previous 10 years from becoming the secretary of defense.

That regulation was changed, however, for one secretary. In 1950, President Harry S. Truman nominated George C. Marshall as secretary of defense. Marshall had retired from a lifelong career in the army only five years earlier. He had then served for 2 years as the secretary of state and was one of the most respected Americans of the era. Truman nominated Marshall at a time when U.S. forces were being sent to South Korea to fight Communist forces of North Korea and China. Truman felt that he

Harry S. Truman

George C. Marshall was the secretary of defense when U.S. troops fought Communist forces in Korea.

needed a defense secretary with military experience. Congress agreed and voted for a one-time exception to the requirement stated in the National Security Act.

USA FACT
The position of secretary of defense has been held by men only, although there is no regulation against a woman serving in the post.

Steps to Approval

Like other members of the cabinet, the secretary of defense is nominated for the position by the president. Once the nomination is made, the person nominated—called the nominee—must appear before the Senate Armed Services Committee. This group of 25 senators interviews the nominee to learn his plans for operating the department. After interviewing the nominee, the committee votes on whether to send the nomination to the full Senate. If the committee approves the nominee, the Senate votes. A nominee who receives a majority vote—more than 50 of the total of 100 senators voting in favor—is approved.

Secretary of Defense Donald Rumsfeld takes the oath of office in 2001.

Once the nominee is approved, or confirmed, he is sworn in. Other civilian nominees for deputy and undersecretary positions also follow the same process before taking office.

USA Fact
No nominee for secretary of defense has ever been rejected by a Senate vote.

Doing the Job

If the Department of Defense were a company, it would be the largest company in the world. It is the nation's largest employer, with more than 3 million military personnel and civilians in its workforce. The department is also responsible for the care and operation of about 250,000 vehicles, more than 15,000 aircraft, and more than 1,000 seagoing vessels.

> **USA Fact**
> Every month the Department of Defense issues 5 million paychecks and pension checks. It makes 920,000 purchases and serves 3.4 million meals.

The top responsibility of running this large organization falls to the secretary of defense. Many of the men who have served as secretary of defense have some military background. Almost all have had experience running large corporations. Being the secretary of defense is much like being a business leader who reports to a chief executive—the president, as well as a board of directors—Congress.

The secretary is responsible for more than 3 million military and civilian personnel and many types of equipment.

A Time of Crisis

Robert McNamara served longer than any secretary of defense—from 1961 until 1968—under Presidents John F. Kennedy and Lyndon Johnson. The most serious problem that faced the country in those years was the war in Vietnam.

For almost 10 years before McNamara took office, the United States had attempted to prevent Communist forces in North Vietnam from taking over South Vietnam. In 1961, several hundred American military advisers were in the country training South Vietnamese troops. Most Americans knew very little about the events taking place there. When the North Vietnamese troops continued to defeat the South Vietnamese, McNamara and Kennedy agreed to send more U.S. military personnel. By 1963—the year Kennedy was assassinated—there were more than 17,000 American troops in Vietnam.

Robert McNamara explained military operations in Vietnam to the press in the 1960s.

American helicopters carried troops to battlefields in South Vietnam.

In 1964, U.S. naval craft off the coast of North Vietnam were reported to have been attacked by North Vietnamese vessels in an area known as the Gulf of Tonkin. Though this report was later said to be false, many Americans were enraged about the attack. In response, President Johnson asked Congress for permission to bomb North Vietnamese cities without formally declaring war. Congress agreed.

Over the next 4 years of McNamara's term, American planes dropped more bombs on North Vietnam than were dropped in World War II. More than 100,000 North Vietnamese were killed. The number of American troops in Vietnam grew to 500,000. Yet South Vietnamese forces continued to suffer defeats.

Throughout the 1960s, growing numbers of Americans protested the war in Vietnam.

McNamara and other American political leaders continued to support American involvement in the Vietnam conflict. By the mid-1960s, however, a growing number of Americans had begun to oppose the war. Antiwar protests and marches took place across the United States. In response to the unrest, the Defense Department and law enforcement agencies secretly began to investigate Americans who spoke out against the war.

By the time McNamara left office in 1968, more than 40,000 American troops had been killed in Vietnam. The American public was now bitterly divided over the war. The fighting did not end overseas until 1975, when the North Vietnamese took control of Vietnam. By then, more than 58,000 Americans had died in the longest war in U.S. history.

Although he defended military action during his term and approved illegal military investigations of Americans, McNamara came to realize that he had failed in this time of crisis. In a book about Vietnam written in 1995, McNamara wrote: "We of the Kennedy and Johnson administrations ... acted according to what we thought were the principles ... of this nation. Yet we were wrong, terribly wrong."

Another Time of Crisis

In 1979, Harold Brown was the secretary of defense under President Jimmy Carter. In November, students and revolutionaries took control of the U.S. embassy in Tehran, Iran. The Iranians took 50 Americans hostage. When diplomatic meetings failed to free the Americans, Brown and Carter gave orders for a military rescue operation. In April 1980, that operation ended in failure when U.S. helicopters and rescue planes collided in the Iranian desert. Eight U.S. servicemen were killed, and the hostage crisis led to Carter's loss of the presidential election later that year to Ronald Reagan.

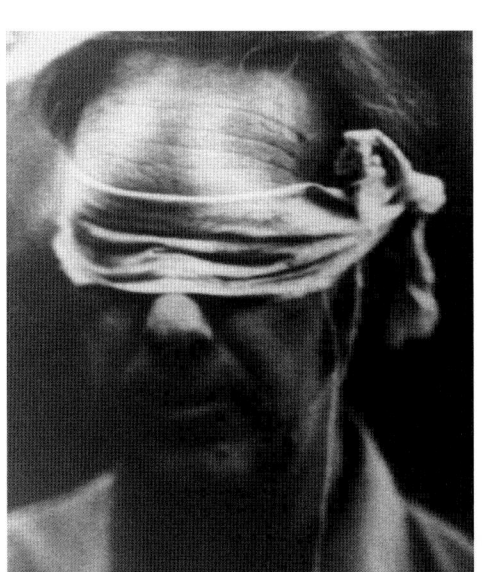

During the hostage crisis of 1979–1980, Americans in Iran were blindfolded and held captive.

A Secretary's Day

The secretary of defense is a busy person whose days are filled with meetings, press briefings, and public appearances. Here is what a day might be like for the secretary of defense.

6:00 AM	Wake, shower, read overnight transmissions from foreign bases, watch television news
6:30 AM	Eat breakfast
7:00 AM	At work in the Pentagon; meet with deputy secretary to preview calendar of events for the day
8:00 AM	Meeting of National Security Council at White House with president, vice president, secretary of state, secretary of the treasury, and national security adviser
10:00 AM	Testify with Chairman of Joint Chiefs of Staff before the House Armed Services Committee on the budget at Capitol
12:00 PM	Interview with host of national radio talk show
1:00 PM	Working lunch with members of Senate Armed Services Committee regarding budget
2:00 PM	Welcome Pakistani president to the Pentagon; discuss military cooperation agreement

Secretary of Defense William Cohen applauds a student following her reading of her award-winning essay, "Women Have Made a Difference."

3:15 PM Appearance at high school to present award to a student writer

4:30 PM Fly to Offut Air Base in Nebraska for dinner honoring service of bomber wing; handle pressing paperwork during 2-hour flight

7:00 PM Speech at dinner honoring air force pilots

8:00 PM Fly back to Washington, D.C.; read briefings of new developments in Middle East

10:30 PM Receive phone call about a training accident in Philippines with casualties; call deputy secretary to schedule press briefing about the accident the following morning

11:00 PM Return home

Fascinating Facts

George Marshall served as secretary of defense from 1950 to 1951. Before that, he served as the secretary of state from 1947 to 1949. In 1953, Marshall was awarded the Nobel Peace Prize for developing a plan to rebuild Europe after World War II.

George Marshall

Two men who served as secretary of defense were presidents of automobile companies before working for the government. **Charles Wilson**, secretary from 1953 to 1957, was president of General Motors. **Robert McNamara**, secretary from 1961 to 1968, was president of Ford Motor Company.

Robert McNamara

Charles Wilson

Donald Rumsfeld

Donald Rumsfeld is the only man to serve 2 different terms as secretary of defense. In 1975, at age 43, he became the youngest man to serve in the position, under President Gerald Ford. In 2001, at age 69, he tied with George Marshall as the oldest man to serve in the position, serving under President George W. Bush.

Elliot Richardson served the shortest term in office, from January until May 1973, under President Richard Nixon.

Richard Cheney is the only man to serve as secretary of defense under one president and as vice president under that president's son. Cheney served as the secretary under George Bush, the 41st president. He then became the vice president under the 43rd president, George W. Bush.

Elliot Richardson

Richard Cheney

Glossary

adviser—a person who works closely with the president and vice president, providing them with information and suggestions

armed services—the 4 separate forces (Army, Navy, Air Force, and Marines) that carry out the military actions of the nation

cabinet—a council of presidential advisers

Congress—the legislative branch of government, composed of the Senate and the House of Representatives

Constitution—the document that established the U.S. government and that contains the principles and laws of the nation

civilian—a person who is not an active member of a military, police, or firefighting force

Department of Defense—a department in the executive branch of government in charge of the armed forces of the nation

National Security Act—an act passed by the government in 1947 that created the position of secretary of defense to be in control of the Department of Defense

National Security Council—a special section of the executive branch that advises the president on matters of national security and foreign policy

nominee—a person who has been proposed to fill a certain position

Oval Office—the office in the West Wing of the White House from which the president works and meets with important people such as the secretary of defense

Pentagon—the government building located in Arlington, Virginia, which houses the Department of Defense

Senate Armed Service Committee—a group of 25 senators who interview the nominees for secretary of defense

and vote on whether to send the nomination to the full Senate for approval

Vietnam War—the military conflict between South and North Vietnam in which the United States was involved for more than 15 years

For More Information

Publications

Aaseng, Nathan. *The White House*. San Diego: Lucent Books, 2000.

Collier, Christopher. *The Middle Road: American Politics 1945-2000*. New York: Benchmark Books, 2002.

Web sites

Office of the Secretary of Defense

http://www.defenselink.mil/pubs/almanac/osd.html

A web site with information on the secretary of defense, his office, and his policies.

U.S. Department of Defense—DefenseLINK

http://www.defenselink.mil

Welcome to the Pentagon

http://www.dtic.mil/ref/html/Welcome/Wlcm.htm

Includes information about Pentagon facilities and services, tours, special points of interest, and the building itself.

Index

antiwar protests 24
armed forces
   air force 6, 27
   army 4, 5, 18
   Coast Guard 10
   marines 10
   navy 4, 5
Armed Services
   Committee 11, 20, 26
assistant secretary
   of defense 12
Brown, Harold 25
Bush, George 29
Bush, George W. 29
cabinet 4, 6, 7, 10, 16, 20
Capitol 14, 16, 26
Carter, Jimmy 25
Cheney, Richard 29
Communist Forces 18, 22
Constitution 4
Congress 4, 6, 7, 11, 18,
                 19, 21, 23
defense agencies 8, 9
Department of Defense 6, 7,
    8, 10, 11, 12, 18, 20, 21, 24

deputy secretary of defense . .12,
                  20, 26
Ford, Gerald 29
Ford Motor Company 28
General Motors 28
government branches
   executive 4, 6, 7, 12
   judicial 4
   legislative 4, 11
House of Representatives 11
Johnson, Lyndon 25
Joint Chiefs of Staff 13, 26
Kennedy, John F. 22, 25
Korean War 18
Marshall, George C. . . .18, 28, 29
McNamara, Robert . . .22-25, 28
National Security Act 18, 19
national security adviser . . .7, 26
National Security Council . .7, 26
Nixon, Richard 29
Nobel Peace Prize 28
Oval Office 16
Pentagon 14, 26
president 4, 7, 10, 12,
                 16, 20, 26

Reagan, Ronald 25
Richardson, Elliot 29
Rumsfeld, Donald 29
secretary of defense
   advisers 12-13, 26, 27
   becoming secretary 20
   office 12, 14, 26
   public appearances 26, 27
   responsibilities 6, 7, 8-11,
     12, 16, 17, 18, 20, 21, 26-27
secretary of state 7, 18, 26
secretary of the navy 5
secretary of the treasury . . .7, 26
secretary of war 4
Senate 11, 20
Tehran, Iran 25
Truman, Harry S. 18
undersecretary 12, 20
Unified Commands 13
vice president 7, 12, 26
Vietnam War 22-25
Washington, D.C. 27
Washington, George 4
Wilson, Charles 28